Paddington

at the
Zoo

First published as a hardback in Great Britain by HarperCollins Publishers in 1984
First published as a paperback edition by Collins Picture Lions in 2000
This edition published in 2010

3 5 7 9 10 8 6 4 2 1

ISBN-13: 978-0-00-786519-2

HarperCollins Children's Books is a division of HarperCollins Publishers Ltd.

Visit our website at: www.harpercollins.co.uk
Printed and bound in China

MICHAEL BOND

Paddington
at the
Zoo

illustrated by R.W. ALLEY

HarperCollins *Children's Books*

One day Jonathan and Judy decided to take Paddington on an outing to the zoo.

Before they set off Paddington made a large pile of marmalade sandwiches – six in all.

But when they reached the zoo, the gatekeeper wouldn't let them in.

"I'm sorry," he said. "Pets aren't allowed."

"Pets!" repeated Jonathan.

"Paddington isn't a *pet*," said Judy. "He's one of the family."

And Paddington gave the man such a hard stare he let them in without another word.

"Come on," said Jonathan. "Why don't I take your picture with the parrot?"

"Give a great big smile," called Judy. "Say cheese!"

"Cheese," said Paddington.

"Squawk!" said a parrot as it took a big bite out of Paddington's sandwich. "Thank you very much. Squawk! Squawk!"

Next they went to see the Siberian Wild Dog.

"Nice doggie," said Paddington.

But the Siberian Wild Dog went, "Owwowwwowwwoo!", and made Paddington jump so much the rest of the sandwich flew out of his hand and landed in the cage.

"Let me take a picture of you with a donkey," said Jonathan.

"Hee! Haw!" brayed the donkey when it saw Paddington's sandwiches.

"That's two gone," said Judy.

Paddington's smile was getting less cheesy all the time.

The elephant didn't wait to be asked
either. It simply made a loud
trumpeting noise –
"Whoooohoowooo!" –
and reached down
with its trunk.

Paddington watched as his third sandwich
disappeared. He began to feel that going to the
zoo was not such a good idea after all.

But there was worse to follow.

When the lion saw them coming, it gave a great roar – "Grrrrrrrrahh!"

It was such a loud roar Paddington dropped his fourth sandwich on the ground and before he could say "help" it was surrounded by pigeons.

The only ones who didn't say anything were the penguins. They just stood there looking sad, as if they were all dressed up for a party but had nowhere to go.

Paddington felt so sorry for them he gave them sandwich number five.

"Penguins eat fish," said a man sternly. He pointed to a notice. "It is strictly forbidden to give them marmalade sandwiches."

And while Paddington was looking at the notice,
the man helped himself to the last
of the sandwiches!

"The cheek of it!" said Jonathan.

"You need eyes in the back of your head," agreed Judy.

"I need my elevenses," said Paddington. "Zoos make you hungry. Besides, nothing more can happen to me now."

But it did. Just to round things off, the mountain goat ate his sandwich bag!

"That does it!" said Jonathan. "If you ask me, it's time we went home."

A few days later Jonathan showed Paddington
the photographs he'd taken at the zoo. "You can
have one for your scrap book," he said.

"Which do you like best?"
asked Judy.

"The one with the parrot," said Paddington
promptly. "At least he said 'thank you'
when he ate my marmalade sandwich.
That's more than any of the others did!"